Nate the Great
and the
Missing Key

Nate the Great

and the

Missing Key

by Marjorie Weinman Sharmat
illustrated by Marc Simont

A YEARLING BOOK

All rights reserved. Published in the United States by Yearling, an imprint of
Random House Children's Books, a division of Penguin Random House LLC,
New York. Originally published in hardcover in the United States by
Coward-McCann, in 1981. Subsequently published in paperback by Yearling,
an imprint of Random House Children's Books, in 1982, and reissued with
Extra Fun Activities, in 2007.

Yearling and the jumping horse design are registered trademarks of
Penguin Random House LLC.

Visit us on the Web! randomhousekids.com

Educators and librarians, for a variety of teaching tools, visit us at
RHTeachersLibrarians.com

Library of Congress Cataloging-in-Publication Data is available upon request.
ISBN 978-0-440-46191-3 (pbk.) — ISBN 978-0-385-37678-5 (ebook)

Printed in the United States of America
82 81 80 79 78 77 76 75 74

First Yearling Edition 1982

Random House Children's Books supports the First Amendment and
celebrates the right to read.

To Mitch,
with love and thanks
for giving me the key
to this mystery
—M.W.S.

I, Nate the Great,

am a detective.

I am not afraid of anything.

Except for one thing.

Today I am going

to a birthday party

for the one thing

I am afraid of.

Annie's dog, Fang.

This morning my dog, Sludge,

and I were getting ready

for the party.

The doorbell rang.

I opened the door.

Annie and Fang were standing there.

Fang looked bigger than ever

and so did his teeth.

But he looked like a birthday dog.

He was wearing a stupid sweater

and a new collar.

"I need help," Annie said.

"I can't find the key to my house.

So I can't get inside

to have the birthday party

for Fang."

I, Nate the Great,
was sorry about the key
and glad about the party.
I said,
"Tell me about your key."
"Well," Annie said,

"the last time I saw it
was when I went out
to get Fang a birthday surprise
to eat."

"To eat?" I said.

"Yes," Annie said.

"Some surprise food.
It's the one present
I had forgotten to buy.
I got Fang lots of presents.
A striped sweater.
And a new collar
with a license number,
a name tag,
a little silver dog dish,
and a little silver bone
to hang from the collar.
See how pretty Fang looks
and hear how nicely he jingles."
I, Nate the Great,
did not want
to look at Fang

or listen to him.

"Tell me more," I said.

"Well, Rosamond and her four cats
were at my house," Annie said.

"She was helping me
get ready for the party.

When I went to the store,

I left Rosamond and the cats

in my house.

I left Fang in the yard.

I left the key to my house

on a table.

That is the last time

I saw the key.

When I got back,

Fang was still in the yard.

But the house was locked,

and Rosamond and her cats

were gone.

Rosamond left this note

stuck to my front door."

Your Key Can Be Found
At A Place That Is Round
A Place That Is Safe
And where Things Are Shiny.
A Place That Is Big
Because It's Not Tiny.
And This Is A Poem.
And I went Home.

"That is a strange poem,"

I said.

"Sometimes Rosamond is strange,"

Annie said.

I, Nate the Great,

already knew that.

"You must go

to Rosamond's house

and ask her

where she put your key," I said.

"I went to her house,"

Annie said. "But it was locked, too.

I rang the bell, but no one was home."

"This is a big day

for Rosamond

and locked doors," I said.

"Who else has a key

to your house?"

"My mother and father.

But they went out for the day.

They don't like dog parties,"

Annie said.

I, Nate the Great,

knew that dog parties

are very easy not to like.

But I said,

"I will take your case."

I wrote a note to my mother.

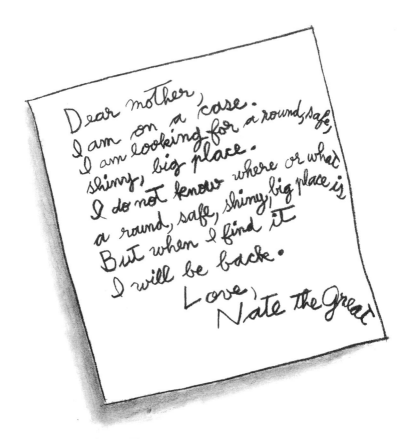

Dear mother,
I am on a case.
I am looking for a round, safe,
shiny, big place.
I do not know where or what
a round, safe, shiny, big place is
But when I find it
I will be back.
Love,
Nate the Great

Annie, Fang, Sludge, and I

went to

Annie's house.

"What does your key look like?"

I asked.

"It is silver and shiny,"
Annie said.

Sludge and I looked around.

There were many places
to leave a key.

Under Annie's doormat.

In her flower garden.

Up her drainpipe.

In her mailbox.

But they were not round,
safe, shiny, and big.

"I will have to look
in other places," I said.

"Fang and I will wait
for you here," Annie said.
I, Nate the Great,
was glad to hear that.

Sludge and I went to Oliver's house.
Oliver is a pest.
But I had a case to solve.
I had a job to do.
I knew that Oliver
collects shiny things.
Like tin cans, safety pins,
badges, poison ivy,
and pictures of the sun.
Each week he collects
one new shiny thing.
Perhaps this week

it was a key.

"Did Rosamond leave a shiny key
with you in a big, round, safe place?"
I asked.

"No," Oliver said.

"This is not my key week.
This is my week
for shiny eels.
Would you like to see
my new eel?"

I, Nate the Great,
did not want to see
a new eel
or an old eel.
I started to leave.

"May I follow you?"

Oliver asked.

"No," I said.

"I will help you look

for the key," Oliver said.

"All right," I said.

"When I go east,

you go west.

When I go south,

you go north."

"But we won't be together,"

Oliver said.

"Exactly," I said.

Sludge and I left Oliver's house.

I did not look back.

I knew what I would see.

Oliver.

I, Nate the Great,
was busy thinking
and looking.
All at once I saw
a big, safe place.
A bank.
I knew there were many
round, shiny things
in a bank.

Like pennies

and nickels

and dimes

and quarters.

Sludge and I walked inside.

Oliver followed us.

Sludge and I looked
on desks and behind counters.
Then we crawled on the floor.
If Rosamond had been here,
there would be cat hairs
all over the floor.

I saw paper clips

and a broken pen

and a penny

and mud.

And a bank guard.

First his feet.

Then the rest of him.

"Do you want

to make a deposit?" he asked.

I, Nate the Great,

wished I could deposit Oliver

in the bank.

I said, "Did anyone strange

with four cats

leave a key here?"

The guard pointed to the door.

Sludge and I left.

Now I, Nate the Great,

knew where I should *not* look

for the key.

A bank was not

a strange enough place

for a strange person like Rosamond

to leave a key.

I had to think of a strange place.

I thought of a kitchen
with bottles of syrup,
hunks of butter,
and stacks of pancakes.
It was not a strange place.
But it was a good place
to think of
because I, Nate the Great,
was hungry.
It was time for lunch.
Sludge and I started for home.

I felt something breathing
on the back of my neck.
I turned around.
It was Oliver.

"I will follow you forever,"
Oliver said.
I, Nate the Great,
knew that forever
was far too long
to be followed
by Oliver.

Sludge and I started to run.

We ran down the street,

up a hill,

around five corners,

and into an alley.

We lost Oliver.

I sat down to rest

beside a garbage can.

Sludge sniffed it.

Sludge likes garbage cans.

I stared at the can.

I had an idea.

A garbage can

would be a perfect place

for Rosamond to hide a key!

It was big and round and shiny

with a shiny cover and shiny handles.
It was safe because no one
would look inside a garbage can.
Except Sludge.
And it was a very strange place
for a key.

Strange enough for Rosamond.
There were not
many places like that.
Now I, Nate the Great,
knew that I had to look
in Annie's garbage can.

Sludge and I walked
to the garbage can
behind Annie's house.
We bent low.
I did not want Annie
to see me
until I found the key
in her garbage can.
Then I would surprise her.
I tried to pull up the cover.
Sludge tried to push up the cover
with his nose.
I pulled harder.
Sludge pushed harder.
The cover came off.
We looked inside the can.

It was empty.
I, Nate the Great,
had not solved the case.
Sludge and I slunk home.
I was very hungry.

I gave Sludge a bone.

I made many pancakes.

I sat down to eat them.

But I did not have a fork.

I opened a drawer.

It was full of spoons and knives

and forks all together

in a shiny silver pile.

I had to pick up

many spoons and knives

before I found a fork.

It is hard to find something

silver and shiny

when it is mixed in

with other things

that are silver and shiny.

I, Nate the Great,

thought about that.

Maybe Annie's key was someplace

where nobody would *see* it

because it was with other

shiny silver things.

A strange place.

A round place.

A big place.

A safe place.

And now I, Nate the Great,

knew the place!

Sludge and I went back

to Annie's house.

Annie was sitting in front

with Fang.

She looked sad.

Fang looked big.

I ran up to Annie.

"I know where your key is,"

I said.

"Where?" Annie asked.

"Look at Fang's collar,"
I said.

Annie looked.

"I see Fang's name tag
hanging from his collar,"
she said. "And his license.
And his silver dog dish.
And his silver bone

and ——————————my key!"

"Yes," I said. "I, Nate the Great,
say that Rosamond hung your key
from Fang's collar.
We did not notice it
because there were other

silver things there."

"But why did Rosamond

hang it there?"

Annie asked.

"Well, it is a very strange place,"

I said. "And remember Rosamond's poem.

A *round* place.

A *big* and *safe* place

where things are shiny.

Well, Fang's collar is round.

The things hanging from it

are shiny.

Fang is big.

And safe.

There is no place

more safe

to leave a key

than a few inches

from Fang's teeth.

No one would try

to take off that key.

Including me."

I started to leave.

"Wait!" Annie said.

She took the key

from Fang's collar.

"Now I can have my party

and you can come!"

I, Nate the Great,
was glad for Annie
and sorry for me.
Just then Rosamond
and her four cats
came up the walk.
"You found the key!"
she said. "I knew
I left it in the perfect place."

I, Nate the Great,
had many things
to say to Rosamond.
But the party was starting.
Annie unlocked the door.

We all went inside.

We sat around the birthday table.

Annie gave me

the seat of honor

because I had solved the case.

It was next to Fang.

I, Nate the Great,

hoped it would be

a very short party.

~ Extra ~
Fun Activities!

What's Inside

NATE'S NOTES: Keys

Most adults carry five to ten keys with them whenever they leave home.

Locks and keys have been in use since about 2000 BC. The earliest ones were made of wood. Before keys became common, people hid their valuables behind moats or on islands surrounded by starving crocodiles.

A dead bolt is a common kind of lock.
When you turn the key in a dead bolt, the
bolt slides into a hole on the doorframe.
Inside the cylinder there is a sort of
puzzle. Only the right key will solve it.
Insert the right key, and its curves and
grooves push up a series of pins the exact
distance necessary to turn the cylinder—
and open the lock!

A remote-controlled lock allows you to open your car door by pushing a button. The "key" transmits a radio signal. Inside the car, a radio receiver gets the message from the "key" to lock or unlock the car.

You can also get a keyless lock for your house. You might press numbers on a keypad to open the lock. Or you might use a plastic card. A really cool keyless lock scans your fingerprint, handprint, or eyeball and then decides whether to let you in.

How many keys exist? To get an idea, think about this: The University of Toronto (in Canada) has more than 100,000 key locks on campus. That's typical for a large university. As Annie discovered, keeping track of keys can be a big job! Still, it's easier than wrestling a starving crocodile or swimming across a moat.

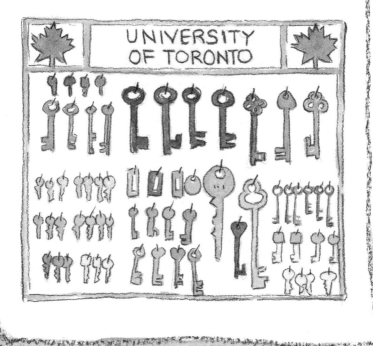

UNIVERSITY OF TORONTO

NATE'S NOTES: Banks

Banks don't like detectives snooping around. Libraries don't mind. So Nate went to the library to find out more about banks.

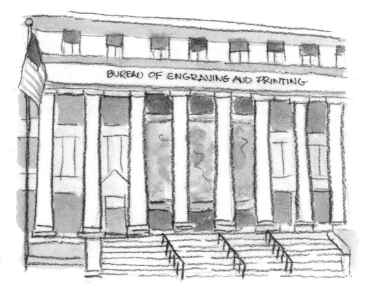

BUREAU OF ENGRAVING AND PRINTING

The U.S. Mint makes pennies, nickels, dimes, quarters, half-dollars, and dollar coins.

Folding money is made at a place called the Bureau of Engraving and Printing.

8

Every coin or bill made by the government shows the year it was issued. (For more about the dollar bill, see pages 10 to 13.)

The vaults of the Federal Reserve Bank on Maiden Lane in New York City store more than one-quarter of the world's gold. The shiny metal is in the form of bars called bullion.

A Map of a Buck

Here's what you'll find on the front of a dollar bill:

A SEAL:
This seal shows which of the twelve Federal Reserve banks issued the bill. "G" stands for Chicago. (The number 7, shown four times, also stands for Chicago.)

A PORTRAIT:
This is George Washi He was the first presi the United States.

TWO SIGNATURES: Each bill shows the signatures of the Treasurer of the United States and the Secretary of the Treasury.

A SERIAL NUMBER:
Each bill has a different
number here.

A SPIDER?
Some people claim to
see a spider here.
Other people say
it's actuallly an owl.
What do you see?

11

Here's what you'll find on the back of a dollar bill:

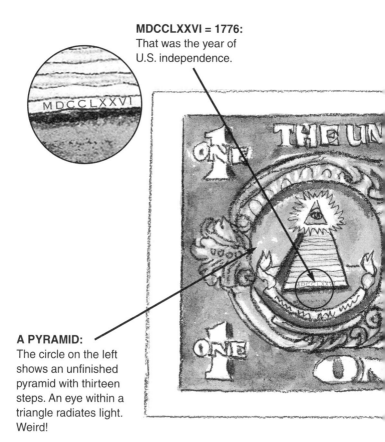

MDCCLXXVI = 1776:
That was the year of
U.S. independence.

A PYRAMID:
The circle on the left
shows an unfinished
pyramid with thirteen
steps. An eye within a
triangle radiates light.
Weird!

THINK INK:
The back of a dollar b[
is printed with green
ink. That's why some
people call dollars
greenbacks.

A BALD EAGLE:
The eagle is the symbol of America. This one holds thirteen olive branches in one foot and thirteen arrows in the other. The branches stand for peace. The arrows mean war.

How to Make a Fancy Dog (or Cat) Tag

*Want to get your dog a present on his birthday?
How about something shiny and round? A new tag!
Cats like them too.*

GET TOGETHER:

- card stock or thin cardboard
- scissors
- a hole punch
- markers
- tinfoil
- clear contact paper
- a key ring

HOW TO MAKE YOUR TAGS:

1. Cut a circle or heart shape out of the card stock or cardboard. Then punch a hole at the top.
2. Decorate one side of the card with a birthday message, like "Happy Birthday" or a drawing of a cake.
3. With a marker, trace the shape onto the tinfoil. Cut it out.

4. Place the shape and the tinfoil together. Enclose them between two pieces of clear contact paper with the sticky sides facing in.
5. Trim the contact paper close to the shape, leaving a little extra on the sides to "glue" the shape and tinfoil together.
6. Clip the tag onto your dog or cat's collar with the key ring.

Funny Pages

Kid: We call our teacher "treasure."
Mom: Why? Do you like her?
Kid: No, we think she should be locked up!

Q: Why did Silly Sam
lock up his pet?
A: *It was a goldfish.*

Q: What happened to a shark that
    swallowed a bunch of keys?
A: *He got lockjaw!*

Q: Why did the football coach go to the bank?

A: *To get his quarterback.*

Q: Why did Silly Sam lock his money in the freezer?

A: *He wanted cold hard cash.*

Q: Where do snowmen keep their money?

A: *In snow banks!*

FROSTY
BANK

How to Make a Present Cake

This cake looks like a really awesome present all wrapped up with a bow. It's nice for a pet's birthday party. Or a person's.

Ask an adult to help you with this recipe.

GET TOGETHER:

- one package of cake mix (any flavor)
- the ingredients listed on the cake mix box
- a sheet cake pan
  (usually 9 inches by 13 inches)
- one can of prepared frosting
- a knife
- Fruit by the Foot
- kitchen scissors

MAKE YOUR PRESENT CAKE:

1. Make the sheet cake by following the directions on the box.
2. Allow the cake to cool for at least one hour.
3. Frost the top of the cake.

4. Wrap your cake in "ribbon": Run a piece of Fruit by the Foot down the center of the cake the long way. Trim to fit with the scissors.

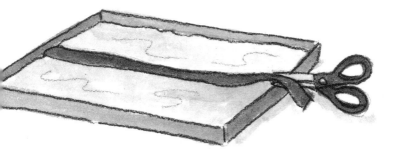

5. Now run another piece of Fruit by the Foot across the width of the cake. Trim to fit. When you're finished, your cake should look something like this:

6. Make the "bow." Use the Fruit by the Foot to make three long loops. You'll need one big one (about as long as your forearm) and two medium ones (about as long as your hand). Put the longer piece in the middle of the other two and squish the centers together like this:

7. Now make two circles, about the size of golf balls. Place the circles on either side of the loops. Run another short piece of Fruit by the Foot around the loops and through the center of each circle so that all the pieces are pulled together, like this:

8. Place the "bow" on top of the cake.

9. Make the ribbon tails. Cut two more pieces of Fruit by the Foot. Cut one end of each into a V shape. Place the plain ends of the ribbon tails under the "bow."

10. Serve while singing "Happy Birthday."

♪ Happy Birthday to You! ♫

11. Enjoy!

More Funny Pages

Doctor, Doctor, Fang's birthday cake gave me heartburn!
Next time don't eat the candles!

Q: What did Fang's birthday party end with?
A: *A Y!*

Q: What does Fang always get on his birthday?
A: *Another year older!*

Q: What do you give Fang on his birthday?
A: *I don't know, but you'd better hope he likes it.*

Q: Why do we put candles on the top of a
   birthday cake?
A: *Because it's too hard to put them on the
   bottom!*

More Ways to Make Your Pet's Birthday Special*

Start the day with a special treat. Is your dog wild about bones? Does your kitty covet liver? Today is the day to go out of your way and provide a yummy breakfast for your furry, feathered, or scaly friend.

Play dress-up. Get into a party mood by putting a bow on your bird's cage or on your fish's aquarium. Your dog or cat may be willing to wear a birthday hat or a special bow on her collar—at least for a few minutes.

Spend a little time. Toss the ball to your retriever, or give your kitty a good belly rub. Make a little extra time for your pet's favorite activity.

Invite a friend. If your pet is the social type, invite a friend to meet you at the park or at your house.

Record the big day. Take photos of your birthday boy or girl. Or make a special piece of art to celebrate the occasion.

*If you don't know your pet's birthday, you can celebrate the day he joined your family!

A word about learning with
Nate the Great

The Nate the Great series is good fun and has been entertaining children for over forty years. These books are also valuable learning tools in and out of the classroom.

Nate's world—his home, his friends, his neighborhood—is one that every young person recognizes. Nate introduces beginning readers and those who have graduated to early chapter books to the detective mystery genre, and they respond to Nate's commitment to solving the case and helping his friends.

What's more, as Nate the Great solves his cases, readers learn with him. Nate unravels mysteries by using evidence collection, cogent reasoning, problem-solving, analytical skills, and logic in a way that teaches readers to develop critical-thinking abilities. The stories help children start discussions about how to approach difficult situations and give them tools to resolve them.

When you read a Nate the Great book with a child, or when a child reads a Nate the Great mystery on his or her own, the child is guaranteed a satisfying ending that will have taught him or her important classroom and life skills. We know that you and your children will enjoy reading and learning from Nate the Great's wonderful stories as much as we do.

Find out more at NatetheGreatBooks.com.

Happy reading and learning with Nate!

Solve all the mysteries with

Nate the Great

- Nate the Great and the Crunchy Christmas
- Nate the Great Saves the King of Sweden
- Nate the Great and Me: The Case of the Fleeing Fang
- Nate the Great and the Monster Mess
- Nate the Great, San Francisco Detective
- Nate the Great and the Big Sniff
- Nate the Great on the Owl Express
- Nate the Great Talks Turkey
- Nate the Great and the Hungry Book Club
- Nate the Great, Where Are You?

MARJORIE WEINMAN SHARMAT has written more than 130 books for children and young adults, as well as movie and TV novelizations. Her books have been translated into twenty-four languages. The award-winning Nate the Great series, hailed in *Booklist* as "groundbreaking," has resulted in Nate's real-world appearances in many *New York Times* crossword puzzles, sporting a milk mustache in magazines and posters, residing on more than 28 million boxes of Cheerios, and touring the country in musical theater. Marjorie Weinman Sharmat and her husband, Mitchell Sharmat, have also coauthored many books, including titles in both the Nate the Great and the Olivia Sharp series.

MARC SIMONT won the Caldecott Medal for his artwork in *A Tree Is Nice* by Janice May Udry, as well as a Caldecott Honor for his own book, *The Stray Dog*. He illustrated the first twenty books in the Nate the Great series.